Tadpoles

Alan and the Animals

by Evelyn Foster

Illustrated by Richard Morgan

Crabtree Publishing Company
www.crabtreebooks.com

Crabtree Publishing Company
www.crabtreebooks.com
1-800-387-7650

616 Welland Ave.
St. Catharines, ON
L2M 5V6

PMB 59051, 350 Fifth Ave.
59th Floor,
New York, NY

Published by Crabtree Publishing in 2011

Series Editor: Jackie Hamley
Editor: Reagan Miller
Series Advisors: Dr. Hilary Minns, Catherine Glavina
Series Designer: Peter Scoulding
Project Coordinator: Kathy Middleton

Text © Evelyn Foster 2010
Illustration © Richard Morgan 2010

Printed in Canada/0207/EF207006

First published in 2010
by Franklin Watts
(A division of Hachette
Children's Books)

The rights of the author and the
illustrator of this Work have
been asserted.

**Library and Archives Canada
Cataloguing in Publication**

Foster, Evelyn, 1964-
    Alan and the animals / by Evelyn Foster ; illustrated
by Richard Morgan.

(Tadpoles)
ISBN 978-0-7787-0573-4 (bound).--
ISBN 978-0-7787-0584-0 (pbk.)

    I. Morgan, Richard, 1942- II. Title. III. Series:
Tadpoles (St. Catharines, Ont.)

PZ7.F81393Al 2011   j823'.914   C2011-900148-9

**Library of Congress
Cataloging-in-Publication Data**

Foster, Evelyn.
    Alan and the animals / by Evelyn Foster ; illustrated
by Richard Morgan.
        p. cm. -- (Tadpoles)
    Summary: Alan, who loves all sorts of animals, has
everything from ten rats to ten wild dogs.
    ISBN 978-0-7787-0584-0 (pbk. : alk. paper) --
    ISBN 978-0-7787-0573-4 (reinforced library binding :
alk. paper)
    [1. Stories in rhyme. 2. Animals--Fiction. 3. Zoos--
Fiction.] I. Morgan, Richard, 1942- ill. II. Title. III. Series.

    PZ8.3.F812Al 2011
    [E]--dc22

                                    2010052355

Here is a list of the words in this story.
Common words:

an	big	in
and	he	

Other words:

Alan	dark	has	ten
animal	dawn	hogs	until
animals	dogs	loves	wild
bats	frogs	park	works
cats	from	rats	

Alan loves animals.

He loves bats!

Alan has ten rats ...

and ten big cats!

Alan loves animals.

11

He loves hogs!

Alan has ten frogs ...

and ten wild dogs!

Alan loves animals, and from dawn until dark ...

Alan works in an animal park!

Puzzle Time

a

b

Can you find these pictures in the story?

Which pages are the
pictures from?

Turn over for the answers!

Answers

The pictures come from these pages:
a. pages 4 and 5
b. pages 18 and 19
c. pages 20 and 21
d. pages 14 and 15

Notes for adults

Tadpoles are structured to provide support for early readers. The stories may also be used by adults for sharing with young children.

Starting to read alone can be daunting. **Tadpoles** help by listing the words in the book for a preview before reading. **Tadpoles** lso provide strong visual support and repeat words and phrases. These books will both develop confidence and encourage reading and rereading for pleasure.

If you are reading this book with a child, here are a few suggestions:

1. Make reading fun! Choose a time to read when you and the child are relaxed and have time to share the story.

2. Look at the picture on the front cover and read the blurb on the back cover. What might the story be about? Why might the child like it?

3. Look at the list of words on page two. Can the child identify most of the words?

4. Encourage the child to retell the story using the jumbled picture puzzle on pages 22-23.

5. Discuss the story and see if the child can relate it to his or her own experiences, or perhaps compare it to another story he or she knows.

6. Give praise! Children learn best in a positive environment.

If you enjoyed this book, why not try another **TADPOLES** story?
Please see the back cover for more **TADPOLES** titles.
Visit **www.crabtreebooks.com** for other **Crabtree** books.